# The Big Splash!

A. H. B. - For Phoebe and Ruby

J. L-S. - To Mum, Dad, Nicky, Elaine Rob, Michelle and Hannah

Written by A. H. Benjamin

Illustrated by Jon Lycett-Smith

All was quiet in the woods...

Hare was enjoying a nibble not far from his house when...

# Da-Dump! Da-Dump! Da-Dump!

The ground shook and shuddered, trees trembled, rocks rattled...

It was a terrible noise!

"It's Shaggybody!" gasped Hare, his long ears quivering nervously.

He didn't even bother to hide and he sprinted off.

Meanwhile, down by the river,
Beaver was admiring the new dam
he had just built when...

# Da-Dump! Da-Dump! Da-Dump!

The ground shook and shuddered, trees trembled, rocks rattled...

It was a terrible noise!

"It's Boulderhead!" s-t-a-m-m-e-r-e-d Beaver, teeth chattering ten to the dozen.

He was off in a flash, his flat tail bobbing up and down.

A little further away, Skunk was frolicking in a flower field to freshen herself up when...

# Da-DUMP! Da-DUMP! Da-DUMP!

The ground shook and shuddered,
trees trembled,
rocks rattled...

It was a terrible noise!

"It's Dreadhorns!" splu-t-t-ered Skunk,
shaking like a leaf.

Scattering flowers left and right, she scampered off as fast as she could.

Deeper in the woods, Raccoon was practising hanging
upside down from his favourite tree when...

**Da-DUMP! Da-DUMP! Da-DUMP!**

The ground shook and shuddered,
trees trembled,
rocks rattled...

It was a terrible noise!

"It's Firenostrils!" wailed Raccoon,
falling from the tree with surprise... Bump!

But he quickly scrambled back to his feet and ran like mad.

Not too far away, Fox was busy
storing food in his secret hideout when...

# Da-Dump! Da-Dump! Da-Dump!

The ground shook and shuddered,
trees trembled,
rocks rattled...

It was a terrible noise!

"It's Thunderhooves!" cried Fox,
frozen to the spot.

But not for long. Forgetting about his precious food, he bolted off.

Soon Hare, Beaver, Skunk, Raccoon
and Fox were frantically running together.

Suddenly, they came to a dead end.

"What do we do now?"
they shouted, panicking.

It was too late to turn back.

Meanwhile, the noise grew louder and more terrible...

# Da-Dump! Da-Dump!

Then, from around the bend, appeared...

... a HUGE, shaggy creature.
His head was the size of a boulder.
His horns were dreadfully long and sharp.

# Da-Dump!

Steam spurted out of his nostrils like fire and
he pawed the ground with thunder-like hooves...

"Hello, everyone!" BOOMED Buffalo cheerfully.
"I thought I'd never catch up with you!"

They all stayed quiet.

"Come on, let's do it!" grinned Buffalo.

"W-we don't want to," they all stammered.
"We saw you do it. I-it's scary...!"

"It's all right," Buffalo reassured them.
"It's fun, you'll enjoy it."

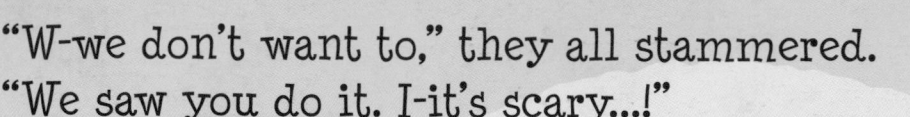

They all looked at each other, thinking long and hard.
At last they plucked up enough courage...

"Oh, all right then," they finally agreed.

One by one they climbed onto Buffalo's back,
and then they were off at a tremendous gallop...

Da-DUMP! Va-VUMP! Da-VUMP!

Past Fox's secret hideout they zoomed...

Under Raccoon's favourite tree they whooshed...

Through Skunk's flower field they ploughed...

Across Beaver's new dam they thundered...

Over Hare's house they bounded...

And still they kept going...

"We're nearly there!" said Buffalo at last.
"Hold on tight, everyone!"

One moment they were running on the ground
and the next they were sailing through the air.

Then there was a BIGGGGGG...

Lift here

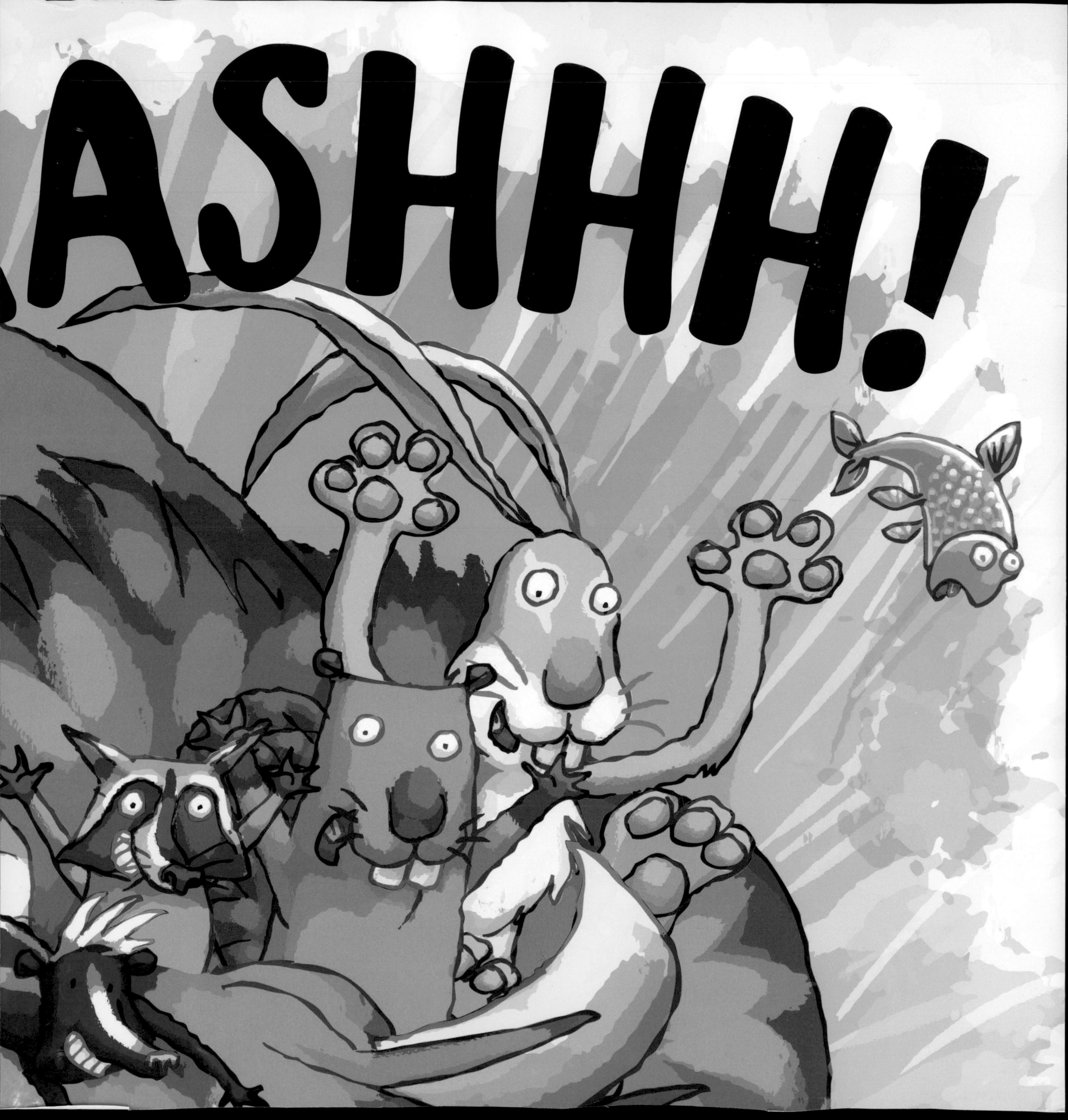
ASHHH!

Shrieks of delight followed as they splashed happily in the warm water of the lake.

"It was scary at first!" they shouted excitedly. "But fun afterwards!"

"I told you so!" laughed Buffalo.

"Shall we do that again?"

"Yes, please!"
they all cried.

First published in Great Britain by Digital Leaf in 2014

ISBN: 978-1-909428-31-7

Text copyright © A.H. Benjamin 2014
Illustrations copyright © Jon Lycett-Smith 2014
The author and illustrator assert the moral right to be identified as the author and illustrator of the work

digital leaf
making stories come to life